GODZILLA
ON MONSTER ISLAND

by Jacqueline Dwyer
Illustrated by Tom Morgan and Paul Mounts

Random House 🏠 New York

Anguirus, Gigan, Godzilla, Kamacuras, Kumonga, Mechagodzilla,
Mothra, Rodan, Varan, and the Character Designs are trademarks of Toho Co., Ltd.

Printed in the United States of America 10 9 8 7 6 5 4 3 2 1

Among the many islands in the vast Pacific Ocean is a special place called Monster Island. It is a tropical paradise of colorful flowers and golden beaches. But people are afraid to visit the island because it is the home of many giant monsters—including Godzilla, the King of the Monsters!

Most of the time, the monsters live together in peace. But Monster Island is small, and sometimes they bump into each other. Then their ferocious roars echo all over the island and wake the mighty Godzilla! When the King of the Monsters bellows in anger, the scared monsters quiet down immediately.

One night, a tropical storm strikes Monster Island. The monsters take shelter from the wind and the rain. They hide inside rocky caves and deep within the thick jungle.

By next morning, the storm is over, and Anguirus and Varan take a walk along the beach. They are surprised to see something huge and round sticking out of the sand. Anguirus wonders what it could be. Did it blow in with last night's storm? Quickly, he runs off to find Godzilla.

The King of the Monsters is taking a nap. Anguirus roars softly in his ear, but Godzilla refuses to wake up. Then Anguirus gently bats him on the nose, but Godzilla simply lets out a long, loud snore!

Finally, Anguirus climbs onto Godzilla's stomach and jumps up and down. Godzilla is angry that anyone would dare to wake him! But he calms down when he sees that it's his friend Anguirus.

Anguirus motions for Godzilla to follow him. Curious, Godzilla lumbers toward the beach.

When Godzilla and Anguirus reach the strange white object, they are surprised to find Kamacuras and Kumonga trying to break it open. The two giant insect monsters are sure there is something good inside to eat.

Kumonga pounds with his eight legs, and Kamacuras bangs hard, too. But the giant white ball will not break.

Suddenly, a blast of scorching air hits their backsides! They spin around as Godzilla lets out another fiery atomic blast. Yikes! Kumonga turns and scuttles up the beach, while Kamacuras takes off with a single flap of his enormous wings.

Godzilla feels a sudden rush of cold air whipping up the sand around him. He looks up to see a helicopter hovering above. Someone is taking pictures of the white ball!

WHACK! A sharp punch knocks Godzilla onto the sand. Stunned, he scrambles to his feet. It's Gigan—one of the meanest monsters ever created.

Gigan lunges toward the strange ball, but Godzilla gets there first. He fires an atomic blast that scorches Gigan's scales. The monster roars and staggers backward. Godzilla fires again. This time, Gigan uses his huge tri-wings to take off into the clouds.

Godzilla and Anguirus guard the strange object for many hours. But the sun is hot, and Godzilla decides to take a swim in the ocean to cool off.

Anguirus watches as Godzilla wades out into the blue water and disappears beneath the surface.

Now Anguirus is left alone on the beach. *Why do I have to watch this boring thing?* he wonders. Suddenly, he spies a tiny crack on its surface. As he watches, another crack appears, then another! Anguirus can't believe his eyes.

Meanwhile, the helicopter that flew over Monster Island lands at a secret floating laboratory. The scientists on board have been studying the monsters for months. Now they want to study the strange white object. They think it is a giant cocoon.

"We must get the cocoon away from the monsters before they destroy it," the head scientist declares. "Prepare Mechagodzilla!"

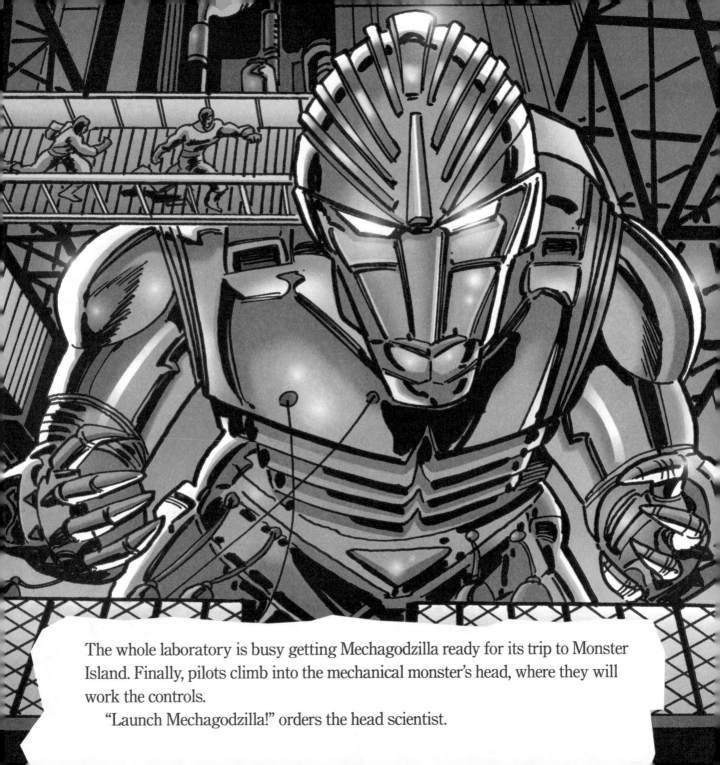

The whole laboratory is busy getting Mechagodzilla ready for its trip to Monster Island. Finally, pilots climb into the mechanical monster's head, where they will work the controls.

"Launch Mechagodzilla!" orders the head scientist.

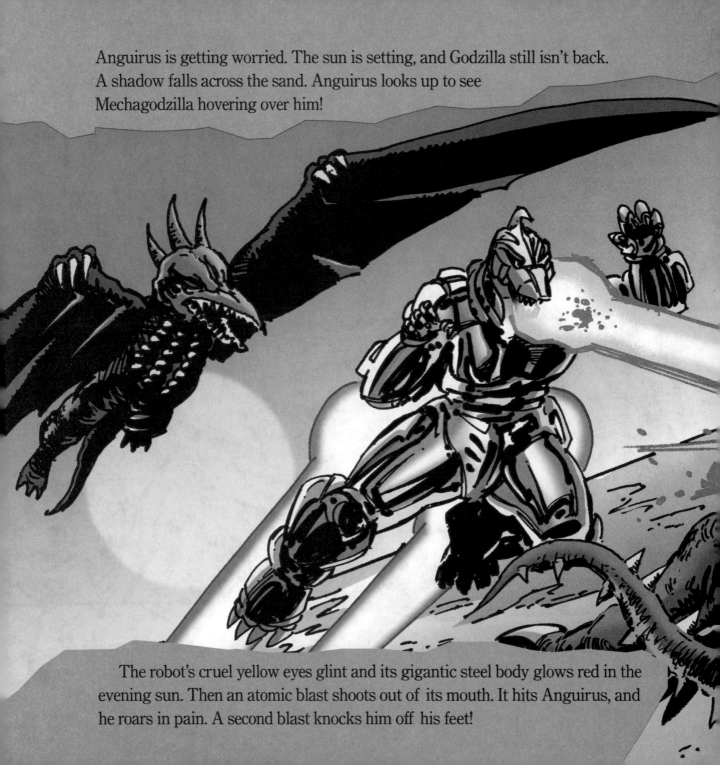

Anguirus is getting worried. The sun is setting, and Godzilla still isn't back.
A shadow falls across the sand. Anguirus looks up to see
Mechagodzilla hovering over him!

The robot's cruel yellow eyes glint and its gigantic steel body glows red in the
evening sun. Then an atomic blast shoots out of its mouth. It hits Anguirus, and
he roars in pain. A second blast knocks him off his feet!

Suddenly, Rodan arrives. He circles the metal beast on his giant wings and pecks at its head. Mechagodzilla lashes out and sends the flying monster tumbling head over talons.

Rodan and Anguirus are no match for Mechagodzilla. They need their friend's help—and fast!

Rodan flies across the ocean. His powerful wings whip up crests of white foam as he skims over the waves. Godzilla bursts to the surface and sees Rodan flapping his wings wildly. Something is wrong!

When Godzilla gets back to Monster Island, he is furious to see Mechagodzilla hurting his friends. He lunges at the metal monster, knocking it off balance. Then Godzilla shoots an atomic blast at the giant robot's chest.

"We're losing power fast," shouts the pilot inside the metal monster. "Let's get out of here!"

Mechagodzilla takes off into the sky, with smoke billowing from its arms and legs.

Whew! That was a close one! the monsters think when Mechagodzilla is out of sight.

A loud crack makes them turn around. The huge cocoon is bursting open! The monsters hold their breath as a colorful giant moth slowly emerges. Her name is Mothra.

Mothra spreads her strong wings and rises into the air. Bright reds, yellows, and oranges glisten and sparkle in the evening sun. The monsters have never seen anything so beautiful.

Mothra gazes down at Godzilla and smiles. A light mist of golden snow begins to fall from her wings. It rains down onto the monsters, filling them with happiness and wonder.

All the monsters gather around Mothra and welcome her into their family. Together, they watch the sun set over the horizon.

Now Monster Island is her home, too.